To the memory of Joanne Taylor, 1952-2010.
A fine writer, a friend and an inspiration. — LL

To my parents, Angela and Ismael. — ÓP

Text copyright © 2015 by Linda Little
Illustrations copyright © 2015 by Óscar T. Pérez
Published in Canada and the USA in 2015 by Groundwood Books

Groundwood Books / House of Anansi Press
110 Spadina Avenue, Suite 801, Toronto, Ontario M5V 2K4
or c/o Publishers Group West
1700 Fourth Street, Berkeley, CA 94710

We acknowledge for their financial support of our publishing program
the Canada Council for the Arts, the Government of Canada through
the Canada Book Fund (CBF) and the Ontario Arts Council.

Library and Archives Canada Cataloguing in Publication
Little, Linda, author
Work and more work / Linda Little ; pictures by
Óscar T. Pérez.
Issued in print and electronic formats.
ISBN 978-1-55498-383-4 (bound). — ISBN 978-1-55498-384-1 (pdf)
I. Pérez, Óscar T., illustrator II. Title.
PS8573.I852W67 2014   jC813'.6   C2014-900970-4
C2014-900971-2

The illustrations were done in pencil on paper, with digital colors,
textures and finishing.
Design by Michael Solomon
Printed and bound in Malaysia

Canada Council
for the Arts

Conseil des Arts
du Canada

ONTARIO ARTS COUNCIL
CONSEIL DES ARTS DE L'ONTARIO
an Ontario government agency
un organisme du gouvernement de l'Ontario

FSC
www.fsc.org

MIX
Paper from
responsible sources
FSC® C012700

WORK
AND MORE
WORK

Linda Little

PICTURES BY

Óscar T. Pérez

GROUNDWOOD BOOKS

HOUSE OF ANANSI PRESS

TORONTO   BERKELEY

Tom worked all morning hoeing turnips.

Every time a dusty traveler or a creaky ox cart passed by, Tom ran out to ask, "Where are you going, mister?" or "Where are you headed, miss?"

"Off to town to sell a pig."

"Down to town to buy a goat."

"Into town to trade a duck for a hen."

Tom sighed and watched as they all disappeared around the bend behind the hill.

"What's it like in the town?" Tom asked his mother.
"It's the same everywhere," she said, never looking up
from her spinning wheel. "Work and more work."

"I'd love to see the town," Tom said to his father.
"There's no point in that," his father said, never
looking up from his anvil where he was shaping nails.
"There's nothing there but work and more work."
Even so, thought Tom, I will go to town.

On the next market day, Tom tied a wee loaf and a bit of cheese into a bundle, kissed his mother and his father and set off down the road.

By and by, he caught a ride on a hay wagon loaded down for market. Soon one road met another, and they passed a church and a forge and a mill, and then there were sheep bleating and people hawking their wares.

"Buy my pots," sang out a boy with a scraggly puppy at his heels.

"Buy my tarts," sang out a woman in a yellow apron.

"You boy," a man called to Tom. "Help me stack these crates on my barge!"

By the end of the day, Tom was tired from working but as happy as he could be. He stretched out on the river barge and shared his supper with the ferryman.

"Where does this barge go?" he asked.

"To the city, of course."

"What's it like in the city?"

"Same as anywhere, I suppose. Work and more work."

Even so, thought Tom, I will go to the city.

Tom had never seen such a hustle and bustle! Up one street and down the next — people and horses and carts, baskets and barrels and boxes, dogs underfoot and birds in cages, everyone hollering and hurrying.

"Ho boy!" a woman called out to Tom. "Run this note up to the parson."

"You there, help me roll these barrels over to the publican."

"Here lad, carry these hinges down to the dockside."

Down at the waterfront, Tom stared at the magnificent ships. Their masts were as tall as church spires, with spars stretched out like arms welcoming those they loved. They had hulls as broad as cottages. Ropes as thick as his legs tied them to the docks.

"What's it like at sea?" he asked a passing sailor.

"Haul the sheets and tend the rigging, boy. It's all work and more work."

Even so, thought Tom as he stared out at the wide ocean, I will go to sea.

The sailors set the sails. The fair winds carried them far out to sea. Tom climbed to the crow's nest at the top of the mast to gaze at the endless blue of a world too vast for his imagination.

When the skies darkened, they sailed through howling winds and waves so wild, Tom feared they would all be lost. But the storms passed.

Just when Tom was sure there was nothing but ocean left in the world, they spied land.

In one port after another, they filled the hold of the ship.

In China, the ship eased its way into port amid a jumble
of crowded sampans and elegant junks.

A fine smoky fragrance drew Tom to a crowded
courtyard. Tea! Great heaping trays of it!

Men hoisted brightly painted tea boxes, one dangling
from each end of their shoulder yokes, and hauled them to
the ship.

In India, the air danced with the aroma of curry and nutmeg. At the market, women brushed by in dazzling saris. Tom saw men stirring dye in a tank with long paddles. Their muscles glistened with sweat in the hot sun.

"Indigo," said a boy with a smile. He handed Tom a small cube of the purest blue — the color of fair sailing.

In Ceylon, the cinnamon peelers sat cross-legged on their mats. They hummed as they peeled thin quills of soft inner bark from cinnamon branches.

Long after the bales of spice were loaded into the hold and the ship sailed away, Tom lay in his hammock and chewed on the fragrant bark, dreaming of the warm green hills of Ceylon.

Tom had been away for a very long time. The wide world was a busy and fascinating place.

Even so, thought Tom, I will go home.

When the ship landed, he made his way back through the city, up along the river to the town (that now seemed very tiny and quiet after all his adventures) and out along the winding road to the little cottage.

"Is it Tom?" his father cried, for Tom was a young man now and quite different from the boy who had left.

"Is it Tom?" his mother cried, for her eyes had begun to dim after all her years of spinning.

"Yes, it's your Tom. With stories and treasures."

The aroma of cinnamon filled the cottage when Tom opened his bundle and spread his gifts across the table.

His father poured boiling water over pinches of Tom's precious tea. His mother reached for the indigo silk and ran it between her rough old fingers. It was as smooth as cream and as blue as forever.

"Everywhere in the world people are busy making beautiful things," Tom said.

"Just as I thought," his father said.

"I told you so," his mother said. "Wherever you go — just work and more work."

BACK IN THE DAYS before engines and electricity, nothing moved that wasn't pushed by air, water, gravity or muscle. Tom lived outside Liverpool in northern England around 1840. By this time the steam engine had been invented, and it was starting to be used to mine coal, run trains and power factories. However, it took a long time to change from the old ways of moving people and goods to the newer ways. By 1840 some goods were being carried to and from ports by trains, but many were still hauled in carts, then loaded onto barges that floated along canals. Tall ships harnessed the wind to sail to distant trading ports. Although people in some parts of the world had begun to move to the cities to work in the new factories run by steam power, many still lived in villages and did a variety of different kinds of work throughout the seasons.

this pointed end to the length he wanted for the nail and set this piece into the bore. The bore had a mold in the shape of a nail head, so when the nail maker hit the nail with one or two quick blows from his hammer, he flattened the top. He repeated this process — sharpening, snipping and hammering — until the entire rod had been made into nails.

IN THE ENGLISH COUNTRYSIDE, one of the jobs women did was to spin sheep's wool. Once the sheep were sheared, the fleeces were washed and carded (combed). Then they were delivered to women who sat for hours a day twisting the fibers together on their spinning wheels. The yarn they made was passed on to weavers, who wove it into cloth on looms. As the nineteenth century wore on, more and more weaving was done in big factories on power looms rather than in weavers' homes on hand looms.

ONE WAY FOR POOR people to earn extra money was by making nails. For this they needed only a hearth with a small, hot fire and a few tools: a hammer, an anvil, a chisel and a special holder called a bore. A supplier would arrive with bundles of thin iron rods for each of his nail makers. The nail maker heated a rod in the fire and pounded one end to a point. Then he snipped off

AT ONE TIME, most of the world's tea came from China. To make tea, people harvested huge sacks of tea leaves and buds and set them out to dry in the sun or breeze. Next they "bruised" the leaves, either a little (by tumbling them in baskets) or a lot (by crushing or tearing them into pieces), and left them in the open air. The more vigorously the leaves were handled and the longer they were left outside, the more they blackened and the more robust the tea's flavor. To stop the blackening, workers seared the leaves in big woks. Then they rolled or kneaded them to bring out their full flavor before baking them. When baking, workers had to be careful not to overcook the leaves.

Finally, packers pressed the tea into wooden boxes for shipping, sometimes using their feet to stomp it down.

NOWADAYS MOST DYES are produced in factories, but long ago, indigo dye came from the leaves of the indigo plant. The indigo plant can grow in tropical climates in many parts of the world, but India once grew and processed most of it. To make the dye, workers soaked the color out of the leaves by fermenting them in a big tank of water. After a day or so, the water turned a dark blue and was poured off into a lower tank. Here the workers stirred it, either with large paddles or by wading up and down in the tank (turning their feet and legs blue!). Then they left it for a little while, and the blue dye simply settled to the bottom. After the water was drained away, the workers scraped the dye off the bottom of the tank. Finally, they dried the dye in the sun and cut it into little cubes to sell.

AT THE TIME OF TOM'S adventures, most of the world's cinnamon came from the small island of Sri Lanka, once called Ceylon. (Most still comes from there!) Cinnamon peeling was a very skilled job that continues to be done by some people today. The peelers would begin by scraping the outer bark off a cinnamon branch. Next, they rubbed the branch all over with a small brass rod that made its surface shiny and loosened its inner bark. Then, very carefully, the peelers made two long incisions along the branch and eased off thin sheets of the soft inner bark. These quills were set in the shade to dry and curl. Next, the peelers telescoped the quills together almost magically into slim poles of cinnamon over a yard (1 m) long. They gathered these into neat, round bales to be transported in ships.